D0463300

Oliver's Box

The Sound of Short O

by Joanne Meier and Cecilia Minden • illustrated by Bob Ostrom

The Child's World

Published by The Child's World®
1980 Lookout Drive
Mankato, MN 56003-1705
800-599-READ
www.childsworld.com

The Child's World®: Mary Berendes, Publishing Director
The Design Lab: Design and page production

Copyright © 2011 by The Child's World®
All rights reserved. No part of this book may be
reproduced or utilized in any form or by any means
without written permission from the publisher.

Library of Congress Cataloging-in-Publication Data
Meier, Joanne D.
  Oliver's box : the sound of short O / by Joanne Meier
and Cecilia Minden ; illustrated by Bob Ostrom.
      p. cm.
  ISBN 978-1-60253-411-7 (lib. bound : alk. paper)
  1. English language—Vowels—Juvenile literature. 2.
English language—Phonetics—Juvenile literature. 3.
Reading—Phonetic method—Juvenile literature. I. Minden,
Cecilia. II. Ostrom, Bob. III. Title.
  PE1157.M548 2010
  [E]—dc22   2010005603

Printed in the United States of America in Mankato, MN.
July 2010
F11538

NOTE TO PARENTS AND EDUCATORS:

The Child's World® has created this series with the goal of exposing children to engaging stories and illustrations that assist in phonics development. The books in the series will help children learn the relationships between the letters of written language and the individual sounds of spoken language. This contact helps children learn to use these relationships to read and write words.

The books in this series follow a similar format. An introductory page, to be read by an adult, introduces the child to the phonics feature, or sound, that will be highlighted in the book. Read this page to the child, stressing the phonic feature. Help the student learn how to form the sound with her mouth. The story and engaging illustrations follow the introduction. At the end of the story, word lists categorize the feature words into their phonic elements.

Each book in this series has been carefully written to meet specific readability requirements. Close attention has been paid to elements such as word count, sentence length, and vocabulary. Readability formulas measure the ease with which the text can be read and understood. Each book in this series has been analyzed using the Spache readability formula.

Reading research suggests that systematic phonics instruction can greatly improve students' word recognition, spelling, and comprehension skills. This series assists in the teaching of phonics by providing students with important opportunities to apply their knowledge of phonics as they read words, sentences, and text.

The letter o makes two sounds.

The long sound of o sounds like o as in: *open* and *rope.*

The short sound of o sounds like o as in: *job* and *box.*

In this book, you will read words that have the short o sound as in: *box, frog, dog,* and *pop.*

Oliver has a box.

He likes to play a game.

Can you guess what
is in the box?

It can hop a lot.

It can jump a lot.

It is a frog!

It is soft.

It can sleep in a box.

Some are named Spot.

It is a dog!

You can drop this.

It will not pop.

It is a balloon!

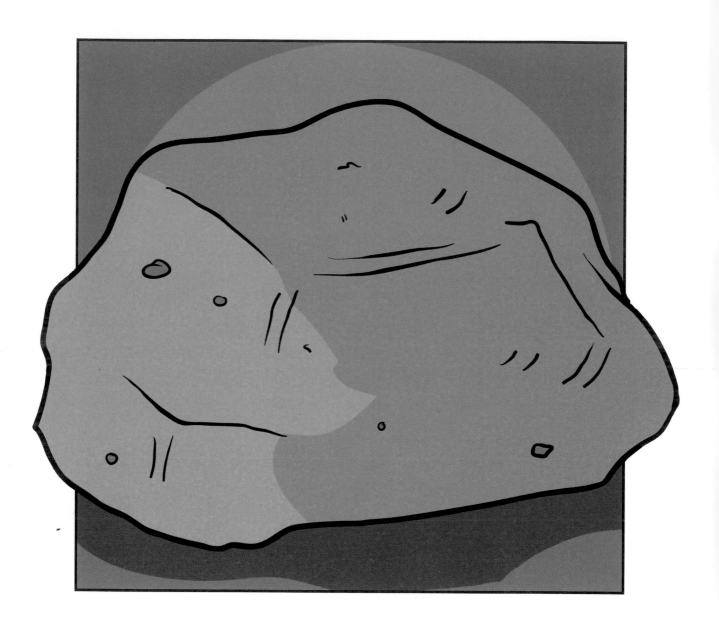

It is not a pet. It is small.

You find it on the street.

It is a rock!

Oliver loves to play this game. You are doing a great job! Keep going!

It can be hot. Mother takes the top off. It is a pot!

Oliver's box has one
more thing. It has hands.
It can tell time. It is a clock!

Oliver loves his box.

You can have a box, too!

What is in your box?

Fun Facts

You might think that most boxes are only used for packing things or for storing your toys. But some boxes can actually make music! The first music box was probably invented in Switzerland in 1770. They were a popular way to play music until the early 1900s, when the phonograph was invented.

The Goliath frog of West Africa is one big amphibian! This frog often grows to be the size of the average house cat. The highest a frog has ever jumped in a single leap is 17.5 feet (5.3 meters). Although frogs have lungs, they actually breathe through their skin. Some kinds of frogs can live to be 40 years old.

Activity

Building a Riddle Box

Are you good at solving riddles? How about your friends? Test your knowledge by building a riddle box. Seal a cardboard box and have an adult help you cut a hole in the top. Write riddles on small slips of paper and drop them through the hole. Have your friends take turns picking riddles out of the box. Whoever answers the most correctly gets to create the riddles that will be used for the next round.

To Learn More

Books
About the Sound of Short O
Moncure, Jane Belk. *My "o" Sound Box®*. Mankato, MN: The Child's World, 2009.

About Boxes
Fleming, Candace, and Stacey Dressen McQueen (illustrator). *Boxes for Katie*. New York: Farrar, Straus and Giroux, 2003.
Portis, Antoinette. *Not a Box*. New York: HarperCollins, 2006.

About Dogs
Beaumont, Karen, and David J. Catrow (illustrator). *Doggone Dogs!* New York: Dial Books for Young Readers, 2008.
Johnson, Bruce, and Sindy McKay. *About Dogs*. San Anselmo, CA: Treasure Bay, Inc. 2009.

About Frogs
Arnosky, Jim. *All About Frogs*. New York: Scholastic, 2002.
Livingston, Irene, and Brian Lies (illustrator). *Finklehopper Frog*. Berkeley, CA: Tricycle Press, 2008.

Web Sites
Visit our home page for lots of links about the Sound of Short O:
childsworld.com/links

Note to Parents, Teachers, and Librarians: We routinely check our Web links to make sure they're safe, active sites—so encourage your readers to check them out!

Short O Feature Words

Proper Names
Oliver
Spot

Feature Words in Medial Position
box
clock
dog
drop
frog
hop
hot
job
lot
not
pop
pot
rock
soft
top

About the Authors

Joanne Meier, PhD, has worked as an elementary school teacher, university professor, and researcher. She earned her BA in early childhood education from the University of South Carolina, and her MEd and PhD in education from the University of Virginia. She currently works as a literacy consultant for schools and private organizations. Joanne lives in Virginia with her husband Eric, daughters Kella and Erin, two cats, and a gerbil.

Cecilia Minden, PhD, is the former director of the Language and Literacy Program at the Harvard Graduate School of Education. She is now a reading consultant for school and library publications. She earned her PhD in reading education from the University of Virginia. Cecilia and her husband, Dave Cupp, live outside Chapel Hill, North Carolina. They enjoy sharing their love of reading with their grandchildren, Chelsea and Qadir.

About the Illustrator

Bob Ostrom has been illustrating children's books for nearly twenty years. A graduate of the New England School of Art & Design at Suffolk University, Bob has worked for such companies as Disney, Nickelodeon, and Cartoon Network. He lives in North Carolina with his wife Melissa and three children, Will, Charlie, and Mae.